BRISTOL CITY COUNCIL
LIBRARY SERVICES
WITHDRAWN AND OFFERED FOR SALE
SOLD AS SEEN

Russell
AND THE
LOST TREASURE

Rob Scotton

1804724921

HarperCollins *Children's Books*

A special thank you to Maria

—R.S.

First published in hardback by HarperCollins Publishers, USA, in 2006
First published in paperback in Great Britain by HarperCollins Children's Books in 2006

3 5 7 9 10 8 6 4 2
ISBN-13: 978-0-00-720625-4
ISBN-10: 0-00-720625-9

HarperCollins Children's Books is a division of HarperCollins Publishers Ltd.
Text and illustrations copyright © Rob Scotton 2006
The author/illustrator asserts the moral right to be identified as the author/illustrator of the work.
A CIP catalogue record for this title is available from the British Library.
All rights reserved. No part of this publication may be reproduced, stored in a retrieval system or
transmitted in any form or by any means, electronic, mechanical, photocopying, recording or
otherwise, without the prior permission of HarperCollins Publishers Ltd,
77-85 Fulham Palace Road, Hammersmith, London W6 8JB.

Typography by Martha Rago

Visit our website at: www.harpercollinschildrensbooks.co.uk

Printed and bound in Singapore

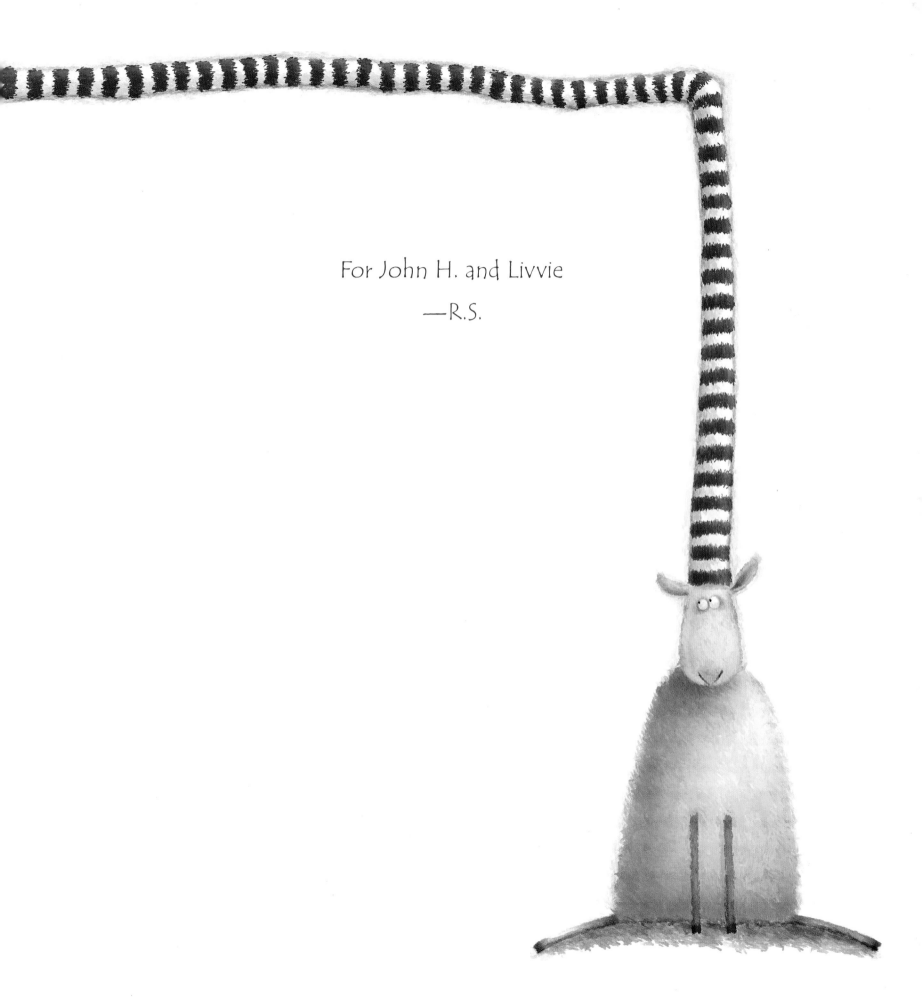

For John H. and Livvie

—R.S.

Russell the sheep was perfecting his triple somersault when...

he was distracted by a passing crow.

"Wow, a treasure map!" exclaimed Russell.

Russell fell to the ground with a thud —
and a really good idea.
   "I will find the Lost Treasure of Frogsbottom!"

So Russell went to his workshop and, after much banging and clattering,

he was ready to
show off his new invention.

"Look out, treasure, here I come!"

He searched high,

he searched low.

He looked in

and out...

over,

under,

left

and right.   Nothing!

WHAT'S
A SHEEP
TO DO?

Russell threw away
the treasure seeker.
It rolled down the hill
and settled at the foot
of a giant tree,
where it began
to beep.

Russell's hat curled with excitement.

He squeezed into a hole
at the base of the tree,

"The Lost Treasure of Frogsbottom!"

Russell dragged the chest
from under the tree,
turned the key

and peered inside.

The chest was crammed FULL, brimming with...

a bunch of useless stuff and a really old camera. "This camera's older than my dad! And I bet it doesn't work!"

"Then again, I bet it does!"

"There is no treasure," said Russell with a sigh. "But maybe we can have some fun anyway."

So he carefully
rummaged through the chest…

...pulled out a painted sheet and tied it between two trees.
"Mum and Dad," he called, "say, 'Fleece!'"

"Granny, put your teeth in. You too, Grandad."

Flash!

Auntie and Uncle wanted a glamorous shot. "Look," said Auntie, "I'm a movie star!"

Flash!

Russell's brother, Cedric, and the cousins wanted an action picture.
"Steady, boys!"

Molly, Polly and Dolly, the triplets, had their photo taken with their dollies — *all of them*.

Russell took Frankie's photo.

Frankie took Russell's photo.

"Cool!"
said Russell proudly.

Russell stuck the photographs into a very big book and sat down to admire his handiwork.

"Hmmm," he thought. "Maybe I have found treasure after all."

"The best treasure ever."